Elizabeth Lee O'Donnell

Patrick's Day

Pictures by
Jacqueline Rogers

Morrow Junior Books   New York

For my nephews
—E. L. O'D.

For Greg
—J. R.

Watercolor and pencil were used for the finished art.
The text type is 17-point Berkeley Old Style Medium.

Text copyright © 1994 by Elizabeth Lee O'Donnell
Illustrations copyright © 1994 by Jacqueline Rogers
Inquiries should be addressed to William Morrow and Company, Inc.,
1350 Avenue of the Americas, New York, NY 10019.
Printed in Singapore at Tien Wah Press.
1   2   3   4   5   6   7   8   9   10

Library of Congress Cataloging-in-Publication Data
O'Donnell, Elizabeth Lee. Patrick's day / Elizabeth Lee O'Donnell ;
pictures by Jacqueline Rogers.   p.   cm.
Summary: Patrick, always well-behaved because he thought
that his town's Saint Patrick's Day parade was in his honor, tries being
naughty like any ordinary boy but finds that he does not like it.
ISBN 0-688-07853-2.—ISBN 0-688-07854-0 (lib. bdg.)
[1. Saint Patrick's Day—Fiction.   2. Identity—Fiction.
3. Behavior—Fiction.   4. Parades—Fiction.   5. Ireland—Fiction.]
I. Rogers, Jacqueline, ill.   II. Title.   PZ7.02386Pat   1994   [E]—dc20   92-27421   CIP   AC

Patrick Murphy sat in the heather. Connell lay beside him. Way up high, clouds scooted. A rainbow climbed the sky. Way down below, the winding streets of the town misted and gleamed.

"Look, Connell," said Patrick. "That's where my parade marches every year."

Connell barked and pushed his nose against Patrick's arm. Patrick scratched the dog's ears. "I've been thinking, Connell. Ever since I was little, my parade has been the same. I'd like to see a change or two. I don't think anybody would mind. After all, it is *my* parade. It isn't for Sean or Brennan or Matthew Lee. And even Da doesn't have a special day all to himself—just me. Patrick's Day."

Connell sneezed and scratched his own ears. Patrick watched the rainbow climb higher. "If you're a special person, Connell, with your own special day, there are certain things you have to do—whether you want to or not. I always go to bed without fussing. I take a bath every day. I help…

"Uh oh, Connell! We've errands to run. I'll race you down into town."

In and out of all the shops he went, Connell at his heels. At the fishmonger's, Patrick whistled O'Flynn's favorite song. O'Flynn sang along just off-key.

"It's not every boy-o who can and will whistle 'The Rising of the Moon' whenever he's asked," said O'Flynn.

Patrick smiled at mean old Mrs. Fitzgibbon, who never smiled at all. She just swung her cane at the ordinary boys who hooted and hollered and spilled down the street.

Patrick patted Mrs. Moran's fat tabby, Mab. "Remember, Connell," he said, "Mab's not for chasing."

Soon the packages were higher than his head. Even
Connell carried one. "We've remembered everything," Patrick
said, walking tall. "And I was proud of you. Mrs. Moran says
you're special, too. Now, what about my parade, Connell? I'm
tired of a just-green parade. Would a little change be too
much to ask? When Da gets home, I'll be asking him."

Before supper, there was the trash to take out, the table to set, the soup to stir. Finally, Da came home. Patrick took his place at the table with Sean and Brennan and Matthew Lee.

"Da," Patrick announced after grace, "I'm tired of green. Tomorrow, let's not have just green in my parade. Let's have a rainbow parade! Let's have blue. And purple and red. And yellow for the sun!"

"*Your* parade?" exclaimed Da. "Dear heart, the parade isn't for you!"

The brothers poked one another and sniggered.

Patrick ignored them. "But it's Patrick's Day," he said. "You told me it was my day and my parade!"

"Patrick Quinn Murphy!" said Mother. "We said nothing of the kind! It's *Saint* Patrick's Day. We said you're named for him. For Saint Patrick, who brought the Word of God to Ireland; who taught with symbols the folk could understand; who— some say—chased all the snakes into the Irish Sea. Green is his color, Ireland's color. The day and the parade honor Ireland's saint, my sweet—not you!"

The brothers laughed so hard, they fell off their chairs.

"Now, boys…" began Mother.

Patrick ran from the house and hid under the spruce tree. Connell snuggled in after him.

"It's a fool I am!" Patrick cried. "I'm not special at all." He wiped his face on Connell's coat. "And if I'm not special, Connell, maybe I'm just…ordinary." He sniffed. "*Ordinary* is for boys who fool and fuss, who holler and whoop. I never tried being ordinary. I don't know what it's like." He squinted his eyes half shut and made fists of his hands. "Let's find out."

Patrick marched into town and sneered at O'Flynn. "I'll never whistle 'The Rising of the Moon' again!" he yelled. "It's dumb!"

O'Flynn was so surprised, he forgot to close his mouth.

Patrick kicked at Mrs. Moran's fat tabby, Mab. He missed and tried again.

Mrs. Moran was so surprised, she forgot to be angry.

Mean old Mrs. Fitzgibbon hobbled by and nodded to him.

"It's an old witch that you are!" Patrick shouted. He jammed his thumbs in his ears, waggled his fingers, and stuck out his tongue.

Mean old Mrs. Fitzgibbon was so surprised, she never noticed a tear slipping down her cheek.

Patrick trudged home. Connell dragged behind. He hung his head and tucked in his tail.

"If you're that ashamed of ordinary me," yelled Patrick, "let someone *special* be getting your supper!"

Patrick burrowed into the dark under the spruce tree.
People went in and out of his house. O'Flynn brought Mrs.
O'Flynn. Mrs. Moran, Mab on her shoulder, marched behind
Mr. Moran and Mr. Solomon from the shop next door.

Mean old Mrs. Fitzgibbon limped in just in front of most of the rest of town. Frowning, they went in; smiling, they came out. Except for Mrs. Fitzgibbon, of course. But she swung her cane snappily.

"They know," said Patrick. "Sean's told them. Everybody knows how dumb I am. Dumb and *ordinary*!" He hunched his shoulders and tried to be smaller.

The sun slipped down behind the far hills.

"Patrick!" Mother called. "It's time to be helping with the dishes."

"Hah!" said Patrick. "I won't. If you're not special, you don't have to help."

A little piece of moon peeped over the rim of the world.

"Patrick!" Mother called. "It's time to be taking your bath and coming to bed."

"Hah!" said Patrick under the spruce tree. "I won't ever go to bed again."

The front door closed with a final-sounding *click*.

"I'm not special," said Patrick, holding on to his mad. "Ordinary boys don't have to be so *very* good."

Somewhere a dog howled. The night wind shooshed. Boughs of spruce whispered and pulled at his hair.

"It's very *big* out here," whispered Patrick.

Something dark flapped and shrieked.

Patrick ran through the yard, up the stairs, and into his room. He dived for his bed.

It was warm. Connell whined and snuggled against him.

"I'm sorry, Connell," Patrick whispered. "Even if I'm not special, you are."

Connell licked his face, and Patrick thought about Mother and O'Flynn. He thought about mean old Mrs. Fitzgibbon and that one tear on her cheek.

"Connell," he said, "I don't like being ordinary. It makes me feel awful." Connell squirmed. "Maybe I don't have to be so *very* ordinary. Maybe I can just be me."

The moon slid down the sky and the sun peered over the rim of the world. Patrick and Connell slipped out of the house. "It's glad I am you're coming with me, Connell. It's hard being brave if you're only ordinary."

The first stop was O'Flynn's. " 'The Rising of the Moon' is a fine song," Patrick said. And he whistled his way through it there and then. "I need a little fish, please," he said when he had done.

At mean old Mrs. Fitzgibbon's, Connell sat down by the gate. "Mrs. Fitzgibbon," said Patrick, "I'm sorry I made you cry. Will you be my friend again?"

Mrs. Fitzgibbon didn't smile, but she winked and sent him on his way.

He hurried on to Mrs. Moran's. "It's very mean I was," he said. "I've brought a fish for your fat tabby, Mab."

At home, everyone was eating breakfast. "It's truly sorry I am," said Patrick. "I didn't know I'm just an ordinary boy. But I promise I won't ever be so very ordinary again."

"Be eating your porridge, our special one," said Da.

"I'm not special," said Patrick. "I'm just me."

Patrick cleared the table and wiped the dishes for Matthew Lee. From down in the town, he heard the bagpipes and drums. It was time for the big parade.

"I don't want to go," he whispered to Connell. "It won't be the same. But even if you're ordinary, there are certain things you have to do—whether you want to or not." And he trailed behind Mother and Da.

"Hurry!" called O'Flynn. "Here it comes!" "Listen to the pipes!" cried Mrs. Moran. Mean old Mrs. Fitzgibbon beat time with her cane.

First came a proud green banner. Great gold letters spelled out ANNUAL SAINT PATRICK'S DAY PARADE.

"Oooh," said Patrick. "I never saw *that* before."

Another banner was next, as blue as midspring skies. It read: FIRST PATRICK'S DAY PARADE.

Everyone cheered. Connell barked. Mab meowed.

"But I'm only *me!*" Patrick cried.

"That's true," said mean old Mrs. Fitzgibbon. "But to all of us, Patrick Quinn Murphy, you're a very *special* me." And she smiled right then and there, for everyone to see.

Mother hugged him tight. Sean and Brennan and Matthew Lee winked and lifted him high.

"You're missing the parade!" Da yelled over the drums' tattoo. "It isn't all green this year."

And it wasn't. For on that fine Saint Patrick's Day, a rainbow marched through town.